Seahaven

The Ravencrest Chronicles
Book One

By

B.K. Bass

Published in the U.S. by B.K. Bass, 2021
Third Edition

Third Edition, 2021

ISBN (Paperback) — 979-8-59-046469-2

Previously published by Kyanite Publishing, 2019
First published by B.K. Bass, 2018

Published by B.K. Bass in the United States of America

Cover and interior art licensed from Dreamstime.com

B.K. Bass can be reached at https://bkbass.com/contact/

For behind the scenes access and the latest news, subscribe to B.K.'s newsletter here: http://eepurl.com/dpaU6f

Visit the author's website at https://bkbass.com

Books by B.K. Bass

<u>The Ravencrest Chronicles</u>
Seahaven
The Hunter's Apprentice
The Giant and the Fishes
Tales from the Lusty Mermaid, a Ravencrest Chronicles Anthology
The Ravencrest Chronicles: Omnibus One
Curse of the Pirate King (The Pirate King Duology: Book One)
Shadow of the Pirate King (The Pirate King Duology: Book Two)

<u>The Night Trilogy</u>
Night Shift
Night Life
Night Shadow

<u>The Tales of Durgan Stoutheart</u>
Warriors of Understone
Companions of the Stone Road (forthcoming)

<u>The Burning Sands</u>
Blood of the Desert
Into the Red Wastes (forthcoming)

<u>Beyond the Veil</u>
Parting the Veil

<u>Standalone Novels</u>
What Once Was Home

Preface to the Third Edition

"Adapt and overcome."

That mantra was drilled into me while I was in the Army. It wasn't just some motivational poster in the recruiter's office or in the barracks at basic training; it was a way of life. The transition from citizen to soldier is all about encountering unfamiliar obstacles and figuring out how to overcome them.

This has probably been one of the two most useful things I learned from the military (the second being "do the right thing"). Throughout the twenty-plus years since I returned to civilian life, "adapt and overcome" has remained an anchor for me no matter what sort of endeavors or obstacles I was engaging with.

Taking the dive into professional writing has been no different.

In fact, I'd say that mantra has served me more often in the last few years than ever before. I hadn't planned to release multiple editions of my books. I had approached them with more of a fire-and-forget mentality. However, unexpected circumstances at several turns have led me to adapt and overcome. These moments have provided opportunities for me to not only grow my skills as an author, editor, and publisher for application to future projects, but also to revisit past projects and apply some extra spit and polish to them.

Which brings us to these pages. Having decided to return to independent publishing, I was granted the opportunity to issue a new edition of this book. While I could have simply updated the numbers and sent it on its merry way, I wanted to come back and spend some more time making sure I was happy with the final result. But, there's been no changes to Gareth's story in Seahaven. I didn't change my mind about a plot point or revamp the pacing. The purpose of this edition, other than the change in publisher, has been to tidy things up. Call it housekeeping, as it were.

Revisiting the pages of my first book has been a joy. I've received a lot of positive feedback on this story over the years, so giving it that extra bit of spit and polish to make sure it really shined felt like the right thing to do.

To both returning guests and new visitors to the city of Seahaven: Welcome! I hope you enjoy your journey, hope to hear what you think of Gareth's story, and hope you'll return to The Ravencrest Chronicles for further adventures!

Seahaven

Chapter One

It was an unusually cold and dark night in Seahaven, only made worse by the deluge of rain. It had poured for days without relenting, and the streets resembled bubbling creeks more than dry-land thoroughfares. The gutters overflowed and refuse from chamber pots ran through the city. The one saving grace of the frigid weather was that the stench of the human waste was not as bad as it would have been on a hot summer day. All but the most dedicated creatures of the shadows were indoors this night; the few intrepid souls who braved the elements dared to defy nature in hopes of fruitful endeavors.

Gareth Vann was one such individual. He had kept his boots dry by remaining above the streets. He stood atop a bell tower, sheltered by the roof of the small gazebo above the bell itself, and looked out over the dark city. Pulling his drab brown cloak close to him to fend off the wind that whipped through the open walls of his perch, he peered out from under a low hanging hood. He wondered if coming out in this awful weather would be worth it this night; perhaps he should have found a warm seat by the fire of his favorite tavern: The Lusty Mermaid.

Shaking thoughts of merriment from his mind, Gareth determined to return his focus to the task at hand. He was out in this rain to make coin, and here he was thinking about spending it before it even jingled in his purse. One gloved hand firmly gripped the railing of the gazebo as he vaulted over to land on the slick roof. He slid along the ceramic tiles, jumped off the edge, and caught a rope stretching to the next building.

The city rulers had a propensity for hanging banners and holding festivals on a regular basis. The purpose was to keep a troubled populace distracted from how horrible their lives really were. The side effect for Gareth was easy travel from roof to roof without ever descending to the rain flooded streets.

The building he came to was a merchant's home, complete with a storefront on the first floor. He landed on a second-floor balcony and peered inside the window. There was a small bedroom with a vanity table, chair, and wardrobe. Upon the vanity sat a mirror of smooth polished glass framed in silver, a sure sign of the merchant's prosperity.

Gareth smiled. When that kind of wealth was sitting out in the open, there was always more hidden away. He tugged at the window and it opened freely, as second-story windows in Seahaven often did. *One of these days*, he thought, *these fools will learn to bar their windows*. That they had not yet was surprising. It wasn't like he was the only footpad in the city, yet his job remained easier than it should have been.

Once inside, he heard the soft snoring of the merchant in his bed. This fellow, Brachus, was an overweight middle-aged man who spent his days carving wood toys for children. On the surface it seemed like an altruistic enterprise, but when one stopped to gauge his prices it seemed he was more concerned with coins than children. Regardless, he was a kindly fellow and his wares were of exceptional quality. Gareth liked the man, but still felt inclined to keep him from getting too fat. In his mind, robbing the merchant was a kindness.

Gareth crept over to the vanity and opened a drawer, finding nothing inside. So, Brachus was learning after all. He moved to the wardrobe next and slowly opened the doors. There was nothing there that would seem ostentatious, however nobody would call them rags. Brachus was well-dressed, but dressed within his station in life. A smart thing to do in this city; one would not want to attract undue attention.

Gareth reached into the wardrobe and pushed the clothing aside. He felt along the back, the top, and the bottom, where his fingers caressed faint grooves in the panel. Pulling a slim stiletto from a sheath in his boot, he slid the blade into the groove and pried open a loose board.

Gareth was rewarded for his persistence, as he found a burlap bag full of coin. It was about the size of his fist; a rewarding bounty, to be sure. He gently slid the bag into a satchel he wore over one shoulder, careful not to let the coins inside make too much noise. He reached back into the compartment and pulled out a small box and two journals. The journals were most likely business ledgers, so he placed them back. Accounting was not of interest to him tonight. He opened the box and felt around inside, finding assorted bits of jewelry. It was probably Brachus' way of consolidating his wealth, but for all Gareth knew, the jewels could also belong to his dead mother. Either way, he didn't want to make a pauper out of the man, so he put the box back. He noticed some shelves on the wall and grabbed a few of the man's carved toys from one of them. They were probably some of Brachus' favorite pieces that he had kept on display. Gareth then snuck silently back out of the room the way he had entered.

He climbed up the timber beams protruding from the plastered wall and pulled himself onto the roof. He could hit another mark or two tonight if he wanted, or he could go find somewhere to dry off. The Lusty Mermaid was clear across town near the docks, and he didn't fancy traveling that far in this weather. Instead, he opted for somewhere closer.

He made his way through the Merchant's Quarter by rooftop, easily jumping from one roof to the other along the rows of tightly packed, two-story buildings. In a city like Seahaven, you had to cram as much as you could into a small space. The city rested between two cliffs in a narrow basin adjacent to the bay. The bluffs dominated the countryside for miles around. Atop one stood the lighthouse, and on the other stood Castle Ravencrest, home of the city's ruler. The Ravencrest family were a reclusive lot and almost never seen in public. Other city officials, many of them fat merchants, ran the day-to-day operations of the city in their stead.

Seahaven rested between those two landmarks, encircled by a twenty-foot-tall stone wall. The city had not been attacked—or even at war—in centuries. The walls were a throwback to a more violent time, but they still served to keep the wolves out; both the kind clad in fur and those who walked on two legs. Gareth didn't consider himself a wolf, by any means. He liked to think he was more like a fox. He took what he needed, and maybe a little extra, but he rarely caused much harm and despised the thought of killing.

Packed shoulder to shoulder within the city walls were the buildings of Seahaven. Many resembled Brachus' home in their wattle and daub construction, and belonged to merchants like the kindly toy carver. Sprawls of single-story hovels built of rough timber planks with thatched roofs dwarfed their number.

More scarce were stone edifices with their own walled lawns and manicured gardens which belonged to the wealthiest residents of the city; many of whom sat on the council. It was these men and women, aristocrats all, who really ran things around here. Gareth would love to see what they had hidden in *their* wardrobes, but he liked his neck the length it was. There was too much to risk being caught in one of those mansions.

He rubbed his neck at the thought and swallowed hard, if only to remind himself that the rope he felt around his neck wasn't real. Hanging, as thieves in the city often were, was a horrible way to die. They would be strung up from permanent gallows affixed over the docks and left there as a message to anybody entering the city by sea. Just to be sure that there was no question why they were being hung, gaolers would cut off their hands before the execution. They were kind enough to tie ropes around the arms of the condemned to make sure they didn't bleed to death before the execution.

Gareth sprung from one roof to the next, struggling not to slip on the wet ceramic tiles. He was eager to get out of the rain to find a warm fire as he reached his destination. He slid down off the edge of the roof and climbed down a beam that had metal pegs driven into it to make for an easy climb. He frequented this place, often arriving the way he just had. The streets still ran thick with rainwater and refuse, so rather than climbing all the way down, he pulled open a window and slid inside.

This was one of his favorite rooms in the building, and one of the few places here that you could find some privacy. There was still a fire burning in the small hearth, and the crackling wood invited Gareth to warm himself. Two high-backed armchairs sat near the fire with their fabric patched in a myriad of colors. They had been a donation, and had been here for almost fifty years; but over time they had been patched and repaired so many times it was hard to tell if anything remained of the original upholstery.

Between the chairs stood a small table, and on it were two steaming clay mugs. A plain, woven straw rug covered the floor, and off to one side of the room there was a simple desk, chair, and bookshelf. The walls were mostly unadorned other than the typical plaster one would expect to see. It was nicked and chipped in many places, although most of the damage was below waist high. There was scribbling on the walls made by the charred end of a stick, as if some mad genius had tried to summon the old gods in a ritual here.

Gareth smiled at the markings, remembering when he used to mark those same walls. "You're going to have to plaster the wall again, Helen."

A soft and frail voice from one of the chairs said, "For as many times as you defaced these walls, Gareth Vann, I should make you do it."

Gareth smiled and removed his cloak, hanging it on a peg by the fire. He sat in the other chair, slid his boots off his feet, and sighed in relief. "You put out some cider for me?"

"Of course," Helen said. The old woman took a sip from her own mug, then set it back down on the table carefully. Her hands shook in her old age, and everything that she did these days had to be deliberate. She was thin and pale; but her skin was still tight, and the wrinkles of time did not betray the true enormity of her age. She wore a simple linen dress dyed a muted olive green. There was no jewelry, no lace, and no paint on her face.

"How did you know I would be here tonight?" Gareth asked. He took a sip from the mug, and the hot apple ale warmed him from within. The liquid soothed his throat, and the alcohol tingled in his belly.

"It was a night like this when you came here the first time, almost thirty years ago. I had a feeling the rain would drive you here."

"I do come here when it's not raining, you know." He took another sip of cider. His pants and coat were wet, and steam rose from them from the heat of the fire.

"True," she admitted, "but when it rains like this, the lost soul yearns for home."

"I brought something for the children," he said, not wanting to continue along those lines. He picked his satchel up from the floor by the fireplace and pulled three of Brachus' carvings from it. One was a wingless dragon, with a long and curving neck and tail. The second was a horseman, complete with shield and lance. The third was a maiden, lovingly crafted and beautiful to behold.

Helen took the carvings, looking at each of them in turn. She seemed to linger on the horseman, rather than the maiden, which surprised Gareth. The woman had quite a past, most of it shrouded in mystery. She loathed to speak of anything from her youth, therefore many of her secrets would be lost in time. "Stolen?"

Gareth huffed, "Acquired."

"Stolen."

"Appropriated."

"Gareth Vann, just because you know fancy words does not mean you are better than any of the other thugs out there. You are a thief, and this is no secret."

"Scolding me again, Helen? Even after I bring you gifts for your children?"

She scoffed at him, setting the carvings down. "If you think you can buy my affection with baubles, you are mistaken."

"What about my charming good looks?" he asked. He had a rugged handsomeness to him, and Helen had never argued that. Dark stubble shaded his square jaw, and his soft eyes spoke of a depth of character most would overlook. His dark hair, tied back into a ponytail, was long and straight. His skin was smooth, as he had never caught the pox.

"Wasted on an old woman like myself, I'm afraid," she sighed. "In another lifetime, maybe." She was touching the lance of the carved horseman lightly, glancing at it with some lost longing in her eyes.

"How are the children?" Gareth asked.

"Have you seen the walls of my sitting room?"

Gareth laughed. The children of the orphanage were lucky to have Helen, just as he was lucky to have found her when he was an urchin, starving on the streets of Seahaven. She had taken him in—as she had many others before and since—and he had grown into a man within these walls.

Chapter Two

Breakfast was amazing in the orphanage, as it always was. Helen had not lost her touch with age. She had help, a cook named Julla, who was young but still knew her way around the kitchen well. Helen had taught her much. Smoked sausages, poached chicken eggs, and a variety of pastries covered the tables. Many would expect orphans to live off a boring diet of porridge or creamed grains, but Helen had always managed to keep her children well-fed. Gareth knew that he helped keep that tradition going with his generous donations of coin. He wondered if—a generation be-fore—some unknown benefactor had kept his belly full as well? Also, was that benefactor formerly a resident like he had been?

Gareth stuffed a pastry covered in sticky lingonberry jam into his mouth. Helen always put just enough sugar in her jams to balance out the tart fruit. He stood, still chewing, and ruffled the red hair of the young waif sitting next to him. The boy looked up and smiled, his cheeks rosy and dotted with freckles. Just a month ago, he had been begging for scraps of bread in the markets. Helen couldn't help every orphan in the city, but she did her best.

Stuffing some biscuits and sausages into his satchel, Gareth strode over to where Helen was pouring out chilled milk into ceramic cups. He kissed her on the cheek, thanking her for the meal.

"Did you sleep at all last night, or did you go back out marauding?" she asked.

"You know I don't maraud," he said with a charming smile, "I *gallivant*."

"Humph," was her only reply as she turned back to her task.

Gareth strode out the front door onto the rain-soaked boards of the front porch. The streets still ran with water, but not as much as the night before. The rain had finally ended, and the sun was trying desperately to peek out through the clouds. If he had any luck, it might even get warm today. He splashed down into the street lightly and made his way through the city. The rain-soaked filth of the city streets ran over his feet, but the calve-high leather boots kept them dry. He kept an eye out in the alleys, searching for members of his network of sparrows.

The typical person doesn't notice a filthy child huddled in the darkness. In fact, many of the well-to-do take pains to avoid them altogether. Making eye contact was a sure way to feel pity for the poor soul, and pity would separate you from your coin. The rich knew even if they didn't let those round eyes convince them to throw a copper bit to the child, those eyes would haunt them after they passed in the form of guilt. This led to a multitude of eyes and ears in the streets attached to virtually invisible little bodies; little bodies that were also adept at getting into places where they did not belong.

Gareth had once been one of those small, invisible, nameless faces. His eyes and ears had picked up on all sorts of things. He had told those things to a man he knew, Kholas; and that man had given him food. In time, Kholas had brought him to Helen. He had still wandered out at all hours of the night, looking and listening, and he had still whispered to Kholas of what he saw and heard. He always had a full belly and a warm bed thanks to Helen, but now he also had a few copper bits thanks to Kholas. He had learned a lot from the man about being where he wasn't supposed to be, opening things he was not supposed to open, and not being seen when he wished to not be seen.

He had passed a lot of this on to his sparrows, including the copper. They saw things, and they heard things, and nobody ever noticed that they were where they should not be. Turning down a narrow alley behind a blacksmith's shop, Gareth found one of his sparrows lounging luxuriously on a pile of straw meant for the smith's donkey. "Comfortable?"

The boy, Miles, opened his eyes, but didn't move to get up. He was about fourteen years old, but already developing the build of a young man. He had a tangled mop of blond hair and pale blue eyes. His feet were bare, and his clothing was simple and torn. "Good enough."

"Hungry?"

At this, the boy sat up. He eyed Gareth suspiciously, but held out a hand nonetheless.

"Nothing's free."

"Well, I guess you'll be giving me something to eat if you want me to tell you the news."

Gareth shook his head, chuckling. "Who taught you to haggle?"

"You did," Miles said, extending his hand again for emphasis. Gareth pulled a sausage from his satchel and handed it to the boy, who took it and bit into it greedily, his mouth full before he even began to chew.

"Well?"

Around a mouthful of the spicy meat, Miles said, "Strange happenings in the noble quarter. Some guards have gone missing at one of the manor houses. The place is pretty much unprotected, if you wanted to go pilfering."

"That's suicide, nobody steals from the nobles without getting their neck stretched."

"Like I said," another bite of sausage, "nobody guarding the place."

Gareth thought on this for a moment. It would be an opportunity to take a huge haul all in one night. On the other hand, if he got caught, he would probably be executed. The idea of that bothered him quite a bit. He had seen too many bodies swinging over the docks in his time, but an unguarded estate was a tempting tar-get.

Miles stuffed the last of the sausage into his mouth, and while still chewing, held out his hand again.

"I already fed you," Gareth said.

"That was a down payment," Miles replied.

Gareth laughed, handed the boy a biscuit, and flipped a copper coin at him. He left Miles to finish his meal in peace and continued on his way. He found a few more of his sparrows as the morning drew on, and all the news was either about the guards disappearing from that manor house or things of a more mundane nature. Nothing else was of any particular interest.

By the time he got home he was out of sausage and biscuits, but not coin. The take from Brachus hadn't been enough to make him wealthy, but his throat wouldn't be dry for some time. Altogether, it was about fifty copper coins and half as many silver pieces, with a handful of copper bits mixed in. He would have liked to have seen some gold in there, but he guessed that Brachus had felt the same way. For as well as the wood carver did, he probably hadn't seen a gold coin himself in years.

Gareth walked up to the simple shack and opened the front door. It wasn't locked. It didn't even *have* a lock. Gareth knew—as well as anybody—that if somebody wanted to open a door, a lock would not stop them. Locks were there to make the wealthy feel safe and to make locksmiths wealthy, and nothing more. The small room he lived in was simple and sparse. There was a small hearth, a straw bed, a table, and one broken chair. He wasn't homeless, but he wasn't far from it. He had probably stolen enough during his life to buy himself a proper house, but he had drunk most of that coin and given the rest to Helen. He did, however, keep a small stash for rainy days.

Gareth pulled a grate, logs and all, out of the hearth. Carefully, he swept the ashes from the fireplace onto a square wood plate and set it aside. Using a slender metal bar, he pried a stone loose from the bottom of the hearth and leaned it against the back of the chimney. Inside, under the hearth, was a small wood box. Again, there was no lock. If somebody found this, then they had earned their pay as far as Gareth was concerned. He opened the box, and inside was a collection of coins and jewelry. There was a little gold in there, but not much. Most of it was silver and copper coins. He dumped a handful out of the bag he had taken last night, keeping out only a few copper coins and a piece of silver. Even with the addition, the contents of the box would barely buy him a horse. He could leave the city if he wanted to, but he'd be poor and have nowhere to go.

That seemed to be the only reason anybody stayed in Seahaven: They were too poor to leave. Except for the wealthy, but what did they have to complain about? Many came to Seahaven with dreams of riches, but the hard truth was that dreams rarely come true. The city was a major trade port and business was always good here. The competition meant that for every successful venture there were at least half a dozen penniless men regretting the decisions they had made in life. Also, the business here was so cutthroat there were another six that had literally had their throats cut.

This was another reason Gareth avoided honest work, as Helen would call it. It didn't matter if you were stealing grain or selling it, somebody in the city wanted you dead. It seemed safer to him to take the approach to prosperity that didn't involve anybody seeing you at work. *Less of a target that way,* he thought. He replaced the box, setting the stone back down in the base of the hearth over it. He took the plate of ashes and dumped them out, scattering them over the stones, and pushed the grate full of logs back into the fireplace.

It looked as though he had not cleaned his hearth in months, just as he intended.

Leaving his hovel, Gareth flashed a smile at some girls walking down the street. They blushed and looked away. He was popular in the neighborhood, but although he had a charming way about him, many knew he was a scoundrel. The local girls all knew his reputation, and though they might smile at him, they were usually interested in more long-term engagements than he offered. Still, it didn't hurt to be friendly.

He lived close to the Merchant's Quarter, so it wasn't out of his way to stop by and see an old friend. It was almost noon, and there were plenty of taverns in that part of town where he could top off his belly before it rumbled. Having grown up on the streets, he had learned to always take advantage of having the time and money for a meal. It wasn't long until the wood plank shacks gave way to the more pristine two-story buildings of the Merchant's Quarter, and the people in the street began to smell better as well. The path was less crowded than usual since the water still flowing over the cobbles was keeping many inside today; but after three days of rain, many people will contend with wet ankles to get out of their homes, stretch their legs, and get some fresh air.

Gareth strode up to his friend's storefront and pulled open the heavy wood door, which rang a tiny brass bell hanging above as it opened. The older man looked up from his work. He had a balding pate with a halo of gray hair, and a chubby face framed with friendly mutton chops. The man smiled and stood, brushing wood shavings from the linen apron he wore over his fine clothing. "Gareth! So good to see you, boy!"

"And you, as well, Brachus," Gareth replied, smiling warmly.

"What brings you in today, another toy for the orphanage, or maybe something to woo the ladies?" Brachus winked, as aware of Gareth's gallivanting ways as the local girls were.

Gareth swatted his arm, then patted the older man on the back heartily. "A toy, I think. I haven't brought one of your carvings to Helen yet this month."

"You are a good man, Gareth Vann, no matter what Helen might say about you."

"And what does she say?" Gareth laughed.

"That you're a tramp, and that you need to marry and settle down."

Gareth rolled his eyes. "She *would* say that. She's just regretting that she's too old for me to bed her."

Brachus guffawed, his face turning red from the effort.

Gareth gave him pause to collect himself, then said, "To business?"

"Yes," the other man said, "and I have just the thing!" He reached under the counter and pulled out a small carved unicorn, carefully painted white with splotches of gray. The horn itself had a pearly shimmer to it.

"How?" Gareth asked.

"The horn? I carved it from the inside of an oyster shell, then stuck it in a hole I drilled in the horse's head. Amazing, isn't it?" Brachus was not reputed for being modest, as one could plainly guess upon first meeting him. His craftsmanship often justified any boast he might offer. The unicorn was exemplary of this, and it was breathtaking.

"It's nice," Gareth said, feigning disinterest to keep the price from going up. "How much?"

"One silver."

"You're proud of your work, aren't you?" Gareth said.

"Of course, if you want something cheaper, I've some scrap wood out back some might call art in the right light."

Gareth fished the silver coin out of his purse—the same one he had taken from Brachus' wardrobe the night before—and set it on the counter. "It'll do," he said.

Brachus smiled, took the coin, and handed over the unicorn. "You confound me, even after all these years."

"Why is that?"

"Because you come in here every month to buy something for Helen's orphanage, complain about the price, and then pay what was asked without blinking. On top of it all, I don't think I've ever seen you do a day of honest work in my life, so I have no idea how you can afford to be so generous."

"Lucky, I guess. I'll see you later. I'm off to see how my luck treats me for the rest of today." With that, he shook the man's hand and left the store. He loved doing business with Brachus, but more than that, he loved giving the man a hard time about his prices. In the end it didn't matter, because he was usually paying the fat merchant with coin stolen from his own bedroom. Gareth enjoyed the irony of that, and his smile grew as he sloshed down the street.

Chapter Three

Standing across the street from the manor house, Gareth still wasn't sure what he was doing there. It would be madness to burgle a house in the Noble Quarter. On the other hand, that maxim was only true because the nobles all had personal guards ensuring that it was so. This might not be true here, given that this home—Hillcrest Manor—had suddenly and mysteriously lost most of their staff.

He pulled his hood down, trying to hide his face. He saw nobody around, but somebody could be watching from the shadows. Just being in this part of town was dangerous. The peasants of Seahaven were not generally welcome in the Noble Quarter, and somebody like him could disappear here with nobody batting an eye. It was rumored that many of the poor who wandered here never were heard from again.

Gareth knew that these stories were exaggerated, and that people liked nothing more than wagging their own tongues for the attention of their peers. The more dramatic the story, the more attention it would garner. Many stories—no matter how outlandish—often had a grain of truth behind them. There were so many stories of people going missing in the Noble Quarter that Gareth was appropriately cautious. He had never heard of an entire household worth of guards disappearing almost overnight. Usually it was one poor soul who had wandered where they didn't belong, not a dozen men who were exactly where they should be.

He looked at the stone wall surrounding the estate, overgrown with vines of ivy. The manor had stood here for generations, built of stones weathered enough to prove it. Usually there would be guards at the gate, which was the only way through the wall, but the only sentries on watch this evening were two stone serpents crouched over either side of the portal.

This night was as dark as last night had been, thanks to the lingering cloud cover. The streets were dry here since this part of the city was high on a hill. Presumably the city's first aristocrats had built their homes far enough away from the harbor that the smell of fish, sweat, and blood did not reach this far. He looked up and down the dark street, lit sporadically by torches and lanterns. In front of Hillcrest Manor itself there was a single lantern by the gate with no candle lit inside, leaving the street shrouded in darkness.

He walked across the street swiftly, drawing a rolled bundle from under his cloak. He threw one end of the rope ladder over the stone wall, and two weighted hooks found a grip on top. He climbed up deftly, drawing the ladder up behind him, and dropped silently down on the other side of the wall.

Luck was still with him, it seemed, as there was nobody inside the wall, either. The manor itself was a two-story building constructed of carved stone blocks, with elaborate round columns and marble arches over the doors and windows. How many backs had been broken building the obscene monolith, nobody knew, but Gareth was sure they had not had the privilege to reside within those walls after their work was done.

He crept across the lawn, passing by well-tended rose bushes and elaborate statuaries. Lily pads bearing white flowers dotted the simple pond at the middle of it all. He noticed that the house itself was dark as he crept up to a first-floor window. Inside was a library, its walls lined in all sorts of books and manuscripts; something you never saw in other parts of the city. He pulled at the window carefully and it swung open. *This is too easy*, he thought.

Gareth climbed inside and looked around the room for anything of value. The books, of course, were worth a fortune by themselves; but who would he sell them to? He couldn't very well push a cart full of books through the Noble Quarter, just hoping that nobody would recognize the volumes stolen from their own shelves. There were candle holders and other accouterments of a library, but nothing made of any metal more precious than brass. He walked to a door and cracked it open.

On the other side was a parlor, and as he looked inside, his eyes brightened along with his hopes. There was a set of silver goblets and a pitcher resting on a platter, and he was sure there was more to find. He slid the goblets into his satchel, leaving the pitcher and platter behind because of their bulk. There was also a writing desk with some bottles of expensive ink, several quills made of exotic feathers, and a gold signet ring with a serpent on it, similar to the statues at the gate. The ring alone might make the night's efforts worthwhile. He considered which room to explore next, examining the three doors leading from the parlor. One lead back to the library, and the other two lead to mystery. He approached the one furthest from the library, an arbitrary decision, and was about to press it open when he heard voices from the other side.

"You must curb your appetites, Gisella," a male voice said. He sounded young and aristocratic, but there was a hint of an accent in his voice that Gareth couldn't place.

"Save me the lecture, Hector. I've seen you do worse," a female voice with a similar accent replied, presumably Gisella.

"Not in our own house, though! And not in this city."

That must be Hector. Gareth looked around, ensuring that he was still alone in the parlor. His instinct was to make his way back out through the library; but the conversation was too interesting, and he could not pull himself away.

"What does it matter, brother?" Gisella asked.

"How can you be so daft? Our home lays unguarded, and the peasants are already spreading rumors about men vanishing from our yards."

"So? Let them talk."

"What of Lord Piotr? How do you think he will react when he hears this?" Hector asked. Gareth realized that the man was speaking of Lord Ravencrest in a manner that made him seem familiar. It seemed natural that they would be associates of the Ravencrest family.

"And how many has *he* killed?" Gisella asked.

How many has Lord Ravencrest killed? Is that what she's asking? Gareth paled.

"This is *his* city, sister, and his chattel to do with as he pleases. We are guests here at Lord Piotr's pleasure, and if you displease him, the consequences will be dire." Again, Hector referred to Gisella as sister. Gareth concluded that they must be siblings, and guests of Lord Ravencrest. He felt like he did as a boy; eyes and ears in the darkness, detecting things they should not be. Only this time, things were much more ominous.

"He can't expect us not to feed," Gisella said flatly.

"He doesn't, but he *does* expect us to exercise some restraint. Go to the Merchant Quarter and suck some poor slob dry. And there is no cause to kill a dozen in one night! That's not feeding; it's just sport."

"But brother, you love the sport as much as I. Don't deny it."

Her voice was seductive, and Gareth couldn't help feeling strangely aroused. The words he was hearing were so disturbing that he decided it was well past time for him to leave.

Gareth turned to make his way back to the library, and that's when his luck ran out. His foot found what must be the one loose board in the entire house, and the floor creaked loudly beneath his feet. He paused in place, his eyes squeezed shut, and cursed himself silently.

"What was that?" Hector asked.

"Hopefully dinner," Gisella said, the eagerness in her tone sending a chill up Gareth's spine.

Gareth ran as fast as he could through the door and into the library. He didn't hear any footsteps behind him, but didn't spare time to turn and check for pursuit. He rolled over the sill of the library window and came to his feet in the same movement, then set off at a run across the yard. The wall still stood between him and the street, and he knew that he was going to lose precious moments trying to climb back out. Still hearing nobody behind him, he chanced a look back.

The man was there, following him. He was close—moving impossibly fast—but seemed to be walking at a leisurely pace. The contradiction between his slow movements and the speed at which he covered ground made Gareth nauseous. Hector bore an all-black suit complete with long-tailed dinner jacket, as if he had just returned from some gala at the castle. The white ruffles on the cuffs of his sleeves half hid his hands, but slender fingers with long nails still extended beyond. He was pale, as if he had been outside little for some years, and his hair was pulled back tight and tied behind him with a red ribbon.

Gareth turned around, after just a momentary glance, and almost ran into Gisella. She had not been there seconds ago, but he now skidded to a halt just before the woman. He fell to his knees in his sudden struggle to stop and looked up at her in awe. She was beautiful in a way that words could never give justice. Her features were slender and angular, yet there were soft curves in all the right places. She was pale like Hector and had bright scarlet hair cascading around her bare shoulders like a fiery waterfall. The red velvet dress she wore had black lace over the bodice, a feature that accentuated her fore-mentioned curves dramatically. The skirts were slit on both sides and revealed more flesh than would be acceptable in polite society. She would have looked like a goddess if not for the unnaturally pale skin and the blood red irises of her eyes. She smiled, showing two elongated canine teeth that would have been at home in the mouth of some nightmare monster than this dreamlike beauty.

Gareth realized he wasn't breathing as he got to his feet and ran perpendicular to his original avenue of escape. A plan for escape ran through his mind. There was a bench in the garden, standing just beneath the wall. If he timed it just right, he could jump from the bench at a run and grab the top of the wall. Then, if he could find a foothold, he should be able to pull himself over.

Another glance over his shoulder showed both Hector and Gisella still giving chase. The man was drifting with no sense of urgency, yet gaining on him. The woman was charging like an angered badger and a hands-breadth from catching him. Gareth leaped onto the bench, kicked off with all his might to grab the top of the wall, and pulled himself over. The thief dropped hard to the street below, rolling several times over the cobbles before he got to his feet, and ran without looking back until he was out of the Noble Quarter. He ran through the Mercantile District, through the market stalls, and past the blacksmith shop. He ran past taverns and brothels. The cold night air burned in his lungs as his heart threatened to break through his ribs. He didn't stop running until he was almost to the harbor, clear across the city from the manor house. He had been running for almost an hour, and his head swam with the exertion. His vision grew blurry as he slowed to a walk. Stumbling, he held onto a wall to keep himself upright. He tried to keep moving, urging his feet one in front of the other.

Finally, he heard bells on the masts of ships moored in the harbor and he knew there was not much further he could go, lest he jump into the sea and swim. He was so tired that he couldn't even bear the thought of taking another step. He collapsed onto a porch of ramshackle wood planks just feet from the door to his destination. As he lay there staring up at the clouds drifting lazily over the moon, he said with a gasping breath, "If they're still after me, they can have me."

Chapter Four

The Lusty Mermaid tavern sat on the docks in the harbor district, half anchored on dry land and half hanging out over the murky waters of the bay. The two-story building looked like it could fall into the harbor at any moment. Light seeped out through cracks between the wood timbers on both floors, and that was where the timbers were not missing. The floor of the main taproom was also missing several boards. It was not rare for a drunken sailor to take a wrong step and end up falling through the floor, one leg hanging precipitously over the chilly waters only ten feet below. There was a deck encircling the establishment, but one had to be very brave or very drunk to go out on those rickety old beams. The second floor housed the rooms of the inn, all furnished with the necessities and often occupied by an assortment of creatures ready to spend the evening with the paying tenants. Chief among them, usually, were fleas.

Gareth had been here for three days since the nightmarish encounter at Hillcrest Manor. He sat alone at a table in the corner of the room, slouched over a flagon of ale. Dark circles ringed his eyes, and his usually close-cropped stubble was growing long and shaggy. Even when the table maid Marcella bent over to drop off another drink, he didn't notice her ample cleavage spilling from the top of her shirt.

She frowned at him. He was usually one of her best customers, both at the tables and upstairs in her bedroom. The last few days he had just sat there nursing his drinks, one after the other. He had taken none of the other women to his room, nor had he come to hers. From the looks of him he hadn't slept in three days, and from the smell he hadn't bathed either. "What's wrong with you, Gareth?"

He looked up sullenly, struggling through the haze of alcohol to focus his eyes. He saw the thick form of a woman in front of him, with curly brunette hair and an empty tankard in her hand. It must be Marcella, but he couldn't make out her face. "Marcella?"

She cocked an eyebrow. "All right, Gareth. You've had enough." She took the tankard she had just dropped off. He tried to reach for it, but was too inebriated to keep up with her. "Go to bed."

Slowly, Gareth stood. He regretted doing so instantly as the Lusty Mermaid spun around him. He held onto the table to steady himself, took a few tentative steps, and then more confidently made his way towards his destination. By the time he got there, he was marching right up to the bar and plopped down on a bar stool. "Jacob," he called out in a slur, "one more for an old friend."

He looked up and realized Marcella was standing behind the bar. He looked around but couldn't find Jacob. She shook her head and pointed towards the stairs. Glumly, Gareth stood and made his way up to the room he had rented. He didn't even bother closing the door as he collapsed onto the bed, alone with his thoughts despite the raucous noise downstairs.

Hector and Gisella had haunted his every waking moment in those three days. He had not slept at all. Every time he closed his eyes, he saw her red eyes staring at him. The unnatural speed and uncanny ease of movement that they both exhibited terrified him. What was worse than all that was the conversation he had heard. Talk of killing, feeding on people, and of the people of Seahaven being chattel for Lord Ravencrest. Nobody knew much about the Duke up in his castle; lord of Seahaven and the surrounding lands, but he normally didn't give the common people cause to question his seclusion.

Now Gareth was questioning a lot of things. He had always felt animosity towards the aristocratic nobles, but purely for economic reasons. He envied their luxurious homes and exquisite clothing. He envied them for not being cold, hungry, or homeless. But since the encounter at the estate, he feared them. He did not understand what was going on, but every possibility he thought of was dreadful. As he pondered these thoughts, he finally slipped into unconsciousness.

*   *   *

Gareth woke well into the next day as the sun glared in through the wavy glass of the room's only window. He raised his hand to shield his eyes and moved to turn over. He forgot that he was not in his own bed and rolled right off the narrow platform and onto the rough floor with a grunt. He laid there for a moment, trying to decide if it was worth the effort to get up.

As he heard heavy footfalls coming down the hall, panic struck him. *They found me*, he thought. *After three days, they finally found me!* Then he remembered that neither Hector nor Gisella had made any sound as they moved, and he relaxed somewhat. Probably just some cutthroat coming to put him out of his misery. He was glad for that.

Hinges groaned in protest as the door swung open.

"Yer a mess," a gruff voice said from the doorway.

Gareth looked up, sighed, and let his head fall to the floor. Now he really wished he was dead. It was Kholas, the onetime benefactor from his childhood. The man stood a good six feet tall, excluding the thick-soled, knee-high black boots he wore with bright blue pants tucked into them. The red shirt above the wide black belt was open almost to the waist, exposing a muscled and hairy chest. The man's gray beard, cut into a sharp cornered square, hung to his collarbones.

He was squinting at Gareth, *but then again, wasn't he always squinting*? Too much time spent in the dark as a youth—he would say if you asked—and too much time in the sun now. The old pirate had a decidedly colorful history, spanning intrigues in the streets of Seahaven to adventures on the high seas, and continued to grow his legacy on the waves.

But now, Kholas stood in Gareth's room, squinting down at the miserable waif that he had picked up from the gutter all those years ago. He kneeled, holding his sheathed cutlass with one hand to keep it from dragging on the floor, and took a closer look at his would-be protégé. "Gareth, get up."

Gareth struggled to raise his head, groaning. He knew better than to defy his old mentor, so he gradually pushed himself up off the floor and sat heavily on the bed. He held his head in between his hands. It was pounding with the beat of a thousand drums, and he wished it would explode and be done with it.

Kholas paced around the room, looking over the filth that the younger man had been wallowing in. Empty bottles, broken crockery, and even a few dried stains from urine decorated the room. He shook his head, wondering what had brought Gareth to this.

"I didn't think you would be in the city," Gareth said, not looking up.

"Docked for some supplies a couple of days ago. Marcella must have recognized the flag and came to get me. Said you were in some sort of trouble."

"You could say that," Gareth said as he walked over to a table by the door, looking for a bottle that wasn't empty. The only thing he could find that had any liquid in it was a clay pitcher of water, probably something Marcella thought he could use. He sniffed at it, decided it smelled clean enough, and turned it over above his head. As the chilly water washed over his body, clothes and all, he felt some of his focus returning.

"Better?" Kholas asked.

"A little," Gareth said, wiping water from his eyes.

"So, you going to tell old Kholas what happened?"

Just like when he was a child, Gareth told Kholas what he had heard and what he had seen. He had done this so many times it felt natural, and it felt good to be talking to his old friend. The pirate's squint grew tight as he listened and digested the words. He didn't seem to want to believe it himself; but admitted he had never seen Gareth so shaken, even as a child. "So, now you're afraid they're after you?"

"Yes, that's why I've been hiding here. I don't dare go back out on the streets," Gareth admitted.

"Did they get that good a look at you? You said it was dark."

Gareth mulled it over for a moment, and thought of how clearly he could see Gisella's face in his mind. "Yes, I'm sure."

"Well then, I guess you've got three options. Either you stay here and drink yerself to death, you jump on my ship with me and leave your troubles behind, or you snap out of it and keep on living until something stops you—like I taught you."

Gareth considered the options. Drinking himself to death was the plan he had been running with, but now that he was more or less sober, he realized that it did not have long-term prospects. Shipping out with Kholas was something that the old man had been trying to talk him into for years now, but he hated boats. He went fishing once with a friend and he threw up the entire time, even though they never left the bay. Getting back to life—it seemed—was the only option that made sense. "What if they come after me?"

"What did I tell you when you too frightened to jump off your first roof?" Kholas asked.

Gareth thought for a moment, then replied, "You said we all die sometime, but the only way to live is to not fear death."

"Aye," Kholas smiled, "and is that any less true now?"

"No," Gareth admitted. He walked over to the older man, shaking his hand. "Thank you for stopping by."

"You better go thank Marcella, if you know what's good fer ya," Kholas said with a chuckle. "She was right fiery, that one was."

Chapter Five

Several weeks went by, and steadily Gareth felt like he was back to his old self. Hillcrest Manor still haunted his dreams, but at least when he was awake, he could focus on what was in front of him. Taking Kholas' advice, he had apologized to Marcella. He returned a few days after that and made it up to her for several hours in her chamber.

Now he was prowling the rooftops again. He had not hit Brachus up for extra change since before he bought the unicorn, but he was going to let the old wood carver have a break for a while. The blacksmith would be a tempting target, but times being what they were, he doubted that there would be much coin there either. On he walked, climbed, leaped, and otherwise scurried his way under the moonlight. After a while, he wasn't sure where he was headed. It felt good to just run the rooftops, not worrying about whys and hows.

He stopped at the edge of one roof and hesitated before he jumped to the next. This road was particularly wide, and there were no lines across which to climb. Looking around, he saw the surrounding buildings were better kept than he was used to seeing. In the distance, a hill rose above him, dotted with walled manor estates.

"Dammit," he cursed himself. In his wanderings, he had come to the edge of the Noble Quarter. This was exactly the place he should be trying to avoid. There, near the top of the hill, he could even make out the silhouette of Hillcrest Manor. What had brought him out this way?

Gareth turned, ready to head back home, and found his path blocked by a hooded figure cloaked all in black. He edged back, almost falling from the roof. He would have; had the figure not reached out a slender, pale hand and grabbed him by the collar. That hand lifted him off the roof with ease. The figure turned around, Gareth still in tow, and walked towards the center of the roof before putting the thief back on his feet. Gareth stared at the person before him, overcome with shock at the uncanny feat of strength, and wondered if he should berate the stranger for startling him or thank him for saving his life.

Just then the figure pulled back the hood of the cloak, revealing the pale and angular features of Hector.

Gareth turned to run, but as he did, he ran into Hector's chest and bounced off, landing on his rear. Unphased, the other man stood perfectly still. He fixed a fold in his cloak with a look of disgust on his face, then said, "She's looking for you."

"Your sister?" Gareth asked, trying to stand up.

"You heard a lot, and you talk too much," Hector said.

"Well, the way I see it, if you were going to kill me, I'd be dead. So, what do you want?" Gareth said defiantly.

"I have use for somebody of your... talents, should we say?" Hector said as he strode around Gareth, seeming to take his measure.

Gareth thought on this for a moment. It made little sense. "Okay, I'll play along. What can somebody like me do for somebody like you?"

Hector smiled, revealing sharp canine teeth just like his sister had. Gareth felt a sudden wave of fear, but stood his ground. Hector nodded and said, "You have eyes and ears all over the city. Information is valuable, is it not?"

Gareth waited in silence, keeping his face neutral as if he were playing a card game.

"Very well," Hector said, "I will speak, you will listen. You will tell your little spies to look for somebody that I want found. This individual is more important to me than you are to my sister. If, say, you were to tell me where he was, I might convince her to forget about you."

"From what I heard," Gareth said, "you're having problems convincing your sister to behave as it is. What makes you think you can talk her into forgetting about me?"

Hector smiled again, "I can be… persuasive."

*   *   *

Hector described the man he was looking for, and Gareth passed this information on to his sparrows. He checked with them day after day, bringing extra bits of copper and boiled eggs to convince them to be more proactive in their searching. He even promised silver to whichever one brought him closer to finding the man in question.

The man that Hector was looking for sounded like an odd fellow, and the aristocrat wasn't willing to tell Gareth why he was so important. The name of the man was Nikolai, and apparently, he was a foreigner newly arrived in the city. That was not unusual for a trade city on the sea, but where he was from was. The kingdom of Dragonspire was a bit of a fable in Seahaven. Old tales said the kingdom derived its name from a dragon-shaped castle carved from the side of a mountain—the seat of the king and the center of their capital city. More ancient ones still spoke of actual dragons residing in those same mountains. Gareth had met nobody from there since it was months of travel overland to reach where it supposedly was. Most visitors came by sea, and if they came by land, it was from farms and villages only a brief ride from Seahaven at most. This man, Nikolai, must have traveled for almost a quarter of a year to get here. Of all the destinations, why would he spend so much time trying to get to Seahaven? And more importantly, why did Hector want him found so badly?

Regardless of the reasons, Gareth continued to search for the man. He knew he wasn't a good man, but he considered himself altruistic in ways. If it came down to his life or a stranger's, however, he was going to look after himself. So, for almost a month, he continued with the same routine day in and day out, always looking over his shoulder. He wondered when Hector would tire of waiting, or if Gisella would find him first. Whenever he saw a woman in a red dress, which was not that often, he ran the other way. His fear was out of control and it was consuming him.

"Gareth," a voice called loudly from an alley.

He jumped with a start, drawing a broad dagger from his belt he had taken to carrying recently. Peering down the alley, he saw a shadowed figure that stood no taller than his shoulder. Swearing, he sheathed the dagger and strode into the alley. "Dammit, Miles!" he admonished, "what have I told you about startling me?"

The boy put a finger to his chin, mocking the deep thought of a scholar. Finally, he answered, "Don't?"

Gareth cuffed him in the back of the head playfully, trying to be mad at the boy, but struggling to find fault in one that was so much like himself in his youth. "What's new?"

Miles held out a hand.

Gareth shook his head, pulling an egg and a crusty roll from his bag and handing them to the youth. "Coin after," he said.

"It'll be a piece of silver today," Miles said around a mouth full of boiled egg.

Gareth's eyes widened, and he pulled the boy deeper into the ally. "You better not be playing me, Miles, or I swear," he trailed off.

"What? You'll gut me with that fish sticker? I doubt it." The boy was unperturbed.

"Tell me what you know," Gareth said.

Miles nodded and held up a finger, working bits of egg yolk out of his teeth with his tongue. He grabbed a bucket from under a rain gutter and took a long swallow of water, then proceeded to tell his news. "So, this foreign guy you are looking for, Nick?"

"Nikolai."

"Yeah, that guy. Word is, he's staying at the Two Fishes Inn, over by the harbor."

"Word is?" Gareth asked, skeptical of second-hand information. The Two Fishes was close to the Lusty Mermaid, and he had been by there often enough that if Nikolai was at the Fishes, he should have found him personally. Also, the man was supposedly a scholar of some sort. Why would he stay in a place like that? If the Lusty Mermaid was exemplary of a disreputable hive of scalawags, the Two Fishes was the bottom of the barrel. Actually, it was more like the scum underneath the bottom of the barrel.

"Word I trust," Miles said, taking a bite of bread, "so it's word you can trust." He held his hand out again.

Gareth untied his purse from his belt, frowning. He didn't like it, but after over a month it was all he had to go on. He fished around to find a piece of silver and pulled it out. The coin had the Ravencrest family seal on one side, a shield emblazoned with a rampant raven framed by a laurel. On the other was a simple outline of Ravencrest castle. He looked at Miles, studying the boy for a moment, then pressed the coin into his hand.

Chapter Six

The condition of the building wasn't all that different from Gareth's usual dive, but it was the patrons that usually kept him away. Thieves and pirates may frequent the Mermaid, but murderers and rapists frequented the Two Fishes. The sign above the door, painted with the image of two fish entangled in the act of procreation, swung in the evening breeze. A light rain pattered on the roof, and Gareth shook the water from his cloak as he stepped onto the covered walkway in front of the inn.

Inside he could hear the sounds of frivolity fueled with plenty of drink. There was a loud crash of splintering wood and a curse, and he could hear shouting from within. He stood beside the door, counting aloud, "One, two, three—" On three, the door swung open and a skinny sailor flew out into the rain-soaked street, blood from his nose mixing with the running water in a swirling cloud of red.

"Evening, Fergus," Gareth said.

The man by the door, Fergus, was a giant of a man. He stood seven feet tall, and almost half as wide at the shoulders. His arms were like tree trunks, and his legs no thinner. He had a broad, flat nose, framed by thin lips and a low sloping brow. He kept his head shaved, likely to show off the octopus tattoo that covered it with its tentacles running down his thickly muscled neck. A large hoop earring hung from one ear. He wore tight-fitting black pants tucked into his boots but was bare chested. "Gareth, I'll be damned. Didn't I say I'd kill you if you ever set foot in here again?"

Gareth smiled, nodding. Fergus was the owner of the Two Fishes and worked there as both bartender and bouncer. He had told Gareth he didn't want anybody else tending the bar so they wouldn't over-pour his liquor, and why would he need a bouncer?

"So, you're here because?" Fergus asked.

"I owe you money," Gareth replied.

"No, that's why you've been staying away. Why are you really here?"

Gareth laughed. Despite his brutish appearance, Fergus was not dim in the wits by any means. "I need to find somebody, and I've heard he's here."

Fergus nodded. "Okay, but you're going to pay me too." It was not a question.

Gareth slipped off a boot and reached inside, balancing on one foot to keep it dry. He pulled two gold coins from the boot, half of all such coin he had saved, and handed it to the big man.

"Interest," Fergus said.

"Damn you, Fergus." He untied his purse again, fished a few coppers out to stuff into his shirt pocket, and tossed the purse over.

Fergus bounced it in his hands a few times and smiled. "It'll do."

They walked inside, and the scent of sweat, piss, and cheap ale struck Gareth. There was a man sitting at a splintered table in the corner nursing a bruised hand. Most likely he was the other half of the dance that had ended with the skinny sailor sleeping it off in the street. Fergus never threw out people for fighting back, just for throwing the first punch. It looked like the little man had made a big mistake, because the other guy looked like he was used to ending fights even if he wasn't in the habit of starting them.

The rest of the crowd all went along the same lines. Sailors, thieves, pirates, and ruffians. Killers, all of them, except for the ones that didn't realize that they were in the wrong place. Gareth was still amazed that his scholarly quarry was staying here, and he thought to himself that Miles had better hope that his trusted information was correct. He wouldn't ever do any permanent harm to the boy, but he wasn't above giving him a good thrashing if he'd been duped.

"Well, here you go," Fergus said, his arms wide.

"He's not here," Gareth said, looking around.

"Well, then, that was a waste of good gold," Fergus laughed.

"Not so fast, friend," Gareth said, "you have rooms upstairs. He's not the type to carouse with your usual clientele."

"Fancy words from mister fancy pants," one sailor said as he passed by. Gareth shot him a threatening glare, and the other man thought better of challenging him.

"Okay, I know who you're talking about. Bookish guy, doesn't want to be bothered," Fergus said.

"That'll be him," Gareth said.

"Doesn't want to be found, either, and paid well for that privilege," Fergus said, crossing his arms. It was back to business again.

"You cleaned me out, Fergus. What more do you want?" Gareth said, holding out his empty hands.

"I'd say you can owe me, but it took you three years to pay off your last debt."

"You know I'm good for it," Gareth jested.

"And you know that I'm impatient," Fergus said.

Mumbling obscene things about Fergus' parentage under his breath, Gareth pulled off the other boot and removed the gold coin he had hidden there. He hadn't realized that saving his own skin would be this expensive, or he might have spent less money on drink over the years. He held out the coin for Fergus to see and said, "After."

"Upstairs, end of the hall on the left. I didn't tell you that. No refunds."

"Agreed," Gareth said, flicking the coin in the air. Fergus scrambled to catch it, cursing as every eye in the taproom followed the motion of the shiny coin.

Flashing currency like that in the Two Fishes would get you killed, even if you were the owner of the place.

Gareth walked to the back of the room and up the stairs, following the directions to his prey. One thing he had not considered was how to get the man to Hector now that he had found him. He was good at stealing things, not people. He realized that he had not really thought this through as he stood in front of the door to Nikolai's room.

He considered knocking, but opted instead to walk in as if he were joining a comrade for dinner. Nikolai was there, pouring over a book at a small table by the light of a single candle. He was middle-aged, with just a hint of gray at the temples and in his sharp pointed beard. He wore plain brown pants and a simple shirt, covered by a woolen vest. He held a small glass lens bound in brass before the book, squinting at the small words through it. A fine chain attached the lens to his vest. He looked up as Gareth entered, smiled, and went back to reading.

Gareth stood there looking at the man. He was dumbstruck by Nikolai's reaction rather than shocking the man. He looked around the room and saw nothing out of the ordinary. He did, however, see a bottle of spirits and a glass. Gareth filled the glass and took a sip of the liquid, convinced that it was of too high a quality to have come from Fergus' usual stock. "Your own bottle?"

"Indeed, my friend. Good to see one with a refined palette in such a dreary hovel," Nikolai said.

Gareth walked over to the table and sat down, noting that having two chairs was rare for a room in the Two Fishes. This Nikolai must have paid well to for such preferential treatment. Gareth felt now Fergus hadn't robbed him, just forced him to outbid Nikolai. "Good book?"

"Indeed."

Gareth sat in silence as the other man read, sipping at the liquor. Lightning flashed outside as rain continued to fall on the city once again. "Lovely weather," he said, breaking the silence, then added, "and if you say indeed, I'll gut you."

Nikolai set the book down with the pages splayed open and placed the looking glass back in his vest pocket. He crossed his hands over one knee and looked Gareth squarely in the eye and said, "Indeed?"

Gareth took a deep breath and sighed. He had been out bluffed before while playing cards, but not with stakes this high. This man was either very smart or very suicidal, and possibly both. "Fine, why are you in Seahaven?"

Nikolai smiled and said, "That's not the question you want the answer to; it's the question that leads to the answer that leads to the question that you want the answer to."

Gareth blinked, staring blankly at the man. He tried to twist his mind around the words, but Nikolai spoke so fast that he couldn't make sense of it. He opened his mouth to say something, but couldn't think of what to say next.

Nikolai got up and walked over to the bed, reaching underneath the straw mattress, and came back with a burlap bundle tied with a thin bit of twine. It was about two feet long, but only a few inches wide. He returned to the chair, laying the bundle across his legs, and said, "To answer your first question, I'm here hunting vampires."

"What is a vampire?" Gareth asked.

"And thus," Nikolai said, "we come to the question that you are looking to get answered, even if you don't know it."

Gareth took another drink, not sure why he was even talking to this man.

"They sent you, didn't they? They can't stand the smell here, you know. Too much humanity in one place, and the nastiest sort at that. This, of course, is why I am staying here."

Gareth spoke up now, "I wondered that. But that still doesn't answer my question."

"Ah, yes: What are vampires? They are not dead, yet not alive. They never eat, yet they must feed. They are beautiful, yet horrifying. They are strong, yet they have a weakness," he said the last softly, running his hand over the bundle in his lap.

Gareth was catching on. He put the pieces of the puzzle together, all the things Nikolai was saying, and looked over at the book. There was an illumination there, a handsome man with pale features, sharp teeth, and blood on his hands. "Hector and Gisella?"

"Indeed," Nikolai smiled, seeing the young thief's mind opening.

"This makes little sense," Gareth said, "how can you be alive and dead, never eat but feed?"

"No," Nikolai retorted sharply, "I did not say alive and dead. I said not dead, yet not alive. Undead."

"Undead?" the word felt strange in his mouth. He had never heard of such a thing.

"Yes, the undead. The creatures whose corporeal bodies have perished, yet their souls refuse to pass on from this world. The vampires are undead, yet they are only one sort of undead. The most nefarious sort, though, if you ask me. They are creatures of the night and bound to it. The sunlight is their bane, and will kill them, so they hunt in the shadows and feed on the blood of the living."

Gareth downed the rest of the glass and got up to refill it. This was all crazy. He didn't believe in any of this kind of talk about souls and passing on. Still, he couldn't explain what he saw that night at Hillcrest Manor. He turned to look at Nikolai, who had a serious expression on his face, but a relaxed posture. He knew that Gareth had been sent to find him by the siblings, but he didn't seem frightened at all. "Why aren't you worried that I'll take you to them?"

"Because, young man, you are more worried about answers than you realize. You have your little network of orphans out there gathering information. You have them all spying and whispering the city's secrets in your ear, and not just since I arrived. It takes years to curate a network such as that, so you've been at this for a while. Therefore, I can assume that you understand the value of information. And to one that understands this, any area where you lack information is frustrating, to say the least. Am I right?"

Gareth stared at the man, the glass in his hand shaking. He blinked once, then threw back the entire thing. "What is that?" he asked, gesturing to the bundle.

Nikolai smiled and untied the twine. He slowly unwrapped the bundle, revealing a short, slender sword of some shiny black material. It seemed forged, or more likely carved, all of one piece. It looked more like stone than metal. The blade was slightly leaf-shaped near the end, but not so much to overweight it. At the base of the blade, a subtle cross guard sat above a slender, leather wrapped handle. At the end, a round pommel finished out the piece. "Obsidian," Nikolai said, running an appreciative hand over the sword.

"The stone?" Gareth asked. He had seen bits of it in jewelry, and even larger pieces used in carvings, but nothing so large.

"Indeed, it is. An exemplary piece, carved by a master mason, then tempered by heating in the fires of a master blacksmith's forge before being cooled in freshly fallen snow. This, my friend, is a work of art. It is also the only sure way to kill a vampire."

"So, you're here to kill Hector and Gisella?" Gareth asked.

"No, I'm not. I'm here to find somebody who can, though," Nikolai smiled.

Gareth opened his mouth to speak, but his throat was suddenly dry. He reached for the bottle and found that it was already empty. He set the glass down and fell into the chair, squeezing the bridge of his nose with two fingers.

"They sent you here to find me, because they knew I was here to find them," Nikolai said.

"And they knew," Gareth said, "that you were looking for somebody to hunt them down?"

"Indeed."

"Will you stop saying that?"

Nikolai frowned and said, "If you insist."

"Never mind, I'm going. You are crazy. They are crazy. I'm crazy if I stay here. I'm going to jump a ship and get the hell out of here." Gareth got up and strode towards the door.

"And Helen? And the children? When they make a meal of them, will you feel no guilt?"

Gareth stopped, hand on the doorjamb. He turned his head to glare at Nikolai.

"Do not hate me, mister Vann. I speak only of what may be. There is nothing to stop them from choosing your former caretaker or her wards as their victims, eventually."

"Why not just tell the city guard, or the council?" Gareth asked.

Nikolai shook his head, "And who runs the guard? Who sits on the council? Do you really believe that these are the only two vampires in this city? Do you doubt that they have ties to the council, or to the Ravencrest family itself?"

"If they aren't the only two, what will killing them accomplish?" Gareth asked.

"Progress, my boy. And the beginning of a new calling. You saw Gisella, as well. Many vampires try to hide by limiting how much they feed. She is lacking in control. She has killed dozens more since you last saw her, compared to a handful by Hector. But, if she is slain, Hector will desire vengeance, so they must both die."

"I'm not so sure," Gareth said. "He almost sounded like he was threatening her."

"Hmm," Nikolai pondered, "that does raise some questions. Maybe, but for another time. He is still a vampire, so the argument is moot. You must kill Gisella, and you might as well kill Hector, as well."

"Wait, wait," Gareth said, holding his hands out before him, "I never said that I was going to do this. You never said you wanted me to do this."

"It was implied," Nikolai said.

"This is crazy, why me?"

"You have a special set of talents, a network of spies, and people whom you care about giving you motivation to see the task done. Also, you have an arrangement with Hector, which will allow you to get close to him."

Gareth opened his mouth to argue, but everything Nikolai said made sense. He turned around, really wishing that bottle weren't empty. He looked down at his hands, coarse and scarred from years of climbing buildings, picking locks, and pilfering trinkets. He wasn't a killer, though. He had been in his share of scraps and even a few knife fights, but he had never killed a man. However, if what Nikolai said was true, these people weren't even alive. "Wait. So, if they're already dead, or not alive, or whatever… how can they be killed?"

"We don't fully understand," Nikolai answered. "There is something about the obsidian that severs not only flesh, but the soul as well. If you wound a vampire with anything but obsidian, they heal unnaturally fast. With the obsidian blade, however, the wound remains." He stood and held the blade out to Gareth. "This may be my war, but this is your city, and your people. We cannot challenge them in the open, but by moving in the shadows we can hunt them down one by one."

Gareth reached out and took the blade, holding it gingerly in his hands. He turned it over, marveling at the smoothness of the stone and the light weight of the sword itself. He thumbed the edge of the blade and found that it was razor sharp. The end, beyond the leaf-shaped curves, came to a sharp stabbing point. The sword would cause a deadly wound to any man, so if Nikolai was right about the vampires, it should be adequate to slay them as well.

Chapter Seven

Gareth stood in the gazebo atop the bell tower with the rain falling around him. The night was reminiscent of a night that seemed so long ago, but was less than two months in the past. His entire view of the world had changed since then. He wore his hooded cloak. He had the steel dagger at his waist and the stiletto in his boot. There was now a leather sheath strapped to his back, and in it was the obsidian sword, hidden easily beneath the cloak—being short as it was.

He looked out over the city, wondering if this might be the last time he would do so. If it wasn't, what would he be doing the next time he stood here? Would he be preparing to hit a mark for coin, or for blood? He sighed, wishing that there was some way he could run from all of this. Nikolai had been right, though. Helen and the children were too precious to him, and he could not leave them to such a horrible fate as being fed upon by those monsters. He didn't know if he could do this, but he had a plan.

He stepped out and started the dance across the rooftops that he had practiced so many times before this night. This part was straightforward. He allowed himself to revel in the freedom, if only for one last time. The raindrops fell on his face as the cold air filled his lungs; he had never felt so alive as he did tonight. He remembered what Kholas had taught him: Keep on living until somebody stops you.

That was going to be the real challenge.

Just as he thought he saw the cloaked figure on the rooftop ahead. He stopped two buildings away from the figure and waited. For several minutes, neither of them made any move. Slowly the figure approached. It was that calm, methodical gait that Gareth recognized from the manor, although the unnatural speed was not apparent. Hector was being deliberate.

Gareth took a deep breath, readying himself. *This is it*, he thought, either this goes as planned, or I die here tonight. He steeled his nerves, trying to look calm. He was sure that the other man could hear his heart pounding in his chest. Nikolai had told him many things after he agreed to take the sword. One of those was that vampires had superior senses, including hearing. Usually this was an advantage, other times a hindrance. Such was the case with the Two Fishes, a place with such a strong smell that they could barely stand to go near it, let alone inside.

"He is not here," Hector said plainly.

"No," Gareth said.

"You met with him, I can smell it," Hector said, his nose wrinkling.

"You knew he was there, didn't you?"

"I suspected," Hector admitted, "but was unsure. I would not want to, as your people say, tip my hand."

Gareth nodded, "Fair enough."

"Why," Hector sounded annoyed, "is he not here?"

"I have a business proposition for you," Gareth said.

Hector's eyes widened, his carefully constructed facade of indifference melting at the sudden surprise. "We had an arrangement, you and I. It seems, however, that you have failed to live up to your end of the bargain."

"I have a new arrangement for you, one that can be mutually beneficial," Gareth said, raising his empty hands either to show he meant no harm, or to plead for Hector's mercy. Even he wasn't sure which.

"I am listening."

"Gisella is out of control. You want her gone, but you can't do it yourself for whatever reason. Honor, family, some vampire law; I don't know why."

Hector hissed at the word vampire; annoyance clear on his face. "A human word, and a nasty one. We prefer to call ourselves immortals."

"Whatever floats your ship, friend," Gareth said, struggling to control his fear, "but back to business. You need Gisella gone, and you don't want Nikolai hunting you down. Am I right?"

Hector nodded.

"Good. Now, that's two things you want. Now, there's two things I want. I want Gisella dead so she won't kill me first, and I want all of you vamp—" he caught himself, "immortals to stay away from the orphanage in the Merchant's Quarter."

"And how, do you presume, will I get the two things that I want?" Hector asked.

"Easy," Gareth said, slowly drawing the obsidian blade. "Nikolai sent me to kill you both. You help me get to her, and I'll tell him I killed you, too. We both get what we want with Gisella, and I get him off your back in return for you getting your kind away from the orphanage."

Hector stood perfectly still, almost too still, for several moments. Finally, he bowed slightly and said, "It is agreed. You will meet me outside of Hillcrest Manor after sunset in exactly one week."

Gareth closed his eyes and sighed in relief. When he opened them, Hector was gone. He stood there for several minutes, catching his breath and collecting his thoughts. He hadn't imagined that would have gone as well as it did. One week, he thought. Either one week to live, or one week until this nightmare was over.

*   *   *

The silver goblet was exquisite, something of genuine beauty in a dark and dreary world. He turned it over in his hand, studying the inlaid carvings. There were men and women dancing, holding jugs of wine and vines of grapes. Their feet bore sandals, and they wore strange robes. He had seen nothing like it before in his life. Oh, he had seen plenty of silver goblets before, but the artwork itself was exquisite. The figures were almost alien to his eyes, like something from another time or another place.

Gareth set the goblets down carefully next to the box beneath the hearth in his home. He had kept them since that night, rather than selling them. At first, he was afraid to have anything to do with them and worried they would lead the hunters to his door. After a while, he grew to appreciate their aesthetic value. Recently, he realized that the artwork was actually a window to another place and time, something these immortals may have carried with them for centuries. This could be the artwork of some long dead civilization. There was no way to know.

He set the stone back into its place and put the hearth back together, ashes and all. He stood, dusting off his pants, and gathered up his things. He touched the purse at his belt, and it felt empty. With everything that was happening around Gareth, he hadn't realized that he was running short on spending coin. He still had what was in the box, but between paying off Fergus and extra grease in the palms of the urchins, even that supply was not what it had been. He stepped out into the night and walked calmly down the street. He didn't have a mark in mind tonight. He had been so distracted he wasn't pressing the children for information or planning any heists. He would just have to wing it, then.

Gareth turned down an alley and hopped easily atop a barrel, reaching up to grab the edge of a balcony. With a little grunting, he pulled himself onto it and from there had an easy climb to the roof. He was on his way again, traveling free of the confines of the city streets.

After a while, Gareth sat perched at the edge of one of the larger markets, looking down at the stalls. They were all empty, their wares taken inside for the night to warehouses or back to the craftsman's homes. There were a few stray potatoes down there, and maybe an onion, but nothing worth the climb. He stood and worked his way around to the other side of the market, when suddenly two hands pushed him from behind.

He fell face first, hurtling two stories down towards the cobbled street. His luck held out, though, and he hit the awning over one of the market stalls first. It tore, but it broke his fall enough that although he hit the ground hard, he was not injured. Gareth groaned, turning over to face up towards the building, and saw a shadowy figure up there. He thought at first that it might be Hector deciding to rescind on their agreement, but the figure was too broad in the shoulder.

Suddenly, the figure jumped from the edge of the building, and seemed to float down to the street level gently, landing with one foot on either side of Gareth. He had a broad face, and although he had angular features, he was by no means attractive. His eyes had those strange red irises, and his skin was pale and wan. He wore the clothing of a well-to-do merchant rather than the fancy garb favored by Hector and his sister. The vampire raised one hand, long fingernails looking like talons, and slashed down at Gareth.

Gareth drew his cloak over himself to block the blow, but those sharp fingernails slashed right through the wool as if it were wet paper. He reached into his boot and drew the stiletto by instinct, driving it into the immortal's thigh. The undead thing wailed in pain and grabbed its leg, giving Gareth time to get to his feet and move out of arm's reach. He drew the obsidian sword from his back and held it out in front of himself, waiting for the vampire's next move.

The larger man pulled the thin dagger from his leg and laughed as he tossed it across the market. There was no blood from the wound at all, and Gareth could see the flesh beneath the torn clothing knitting back together. Still laughing, the vampire charged at him with both talon-like hands upraised.

Gareth charged back, roaring a cry that expressed a mixture of anger and fear. He thought maybe that's what a war cry was supposed to be, but he really didn't know. In a half-dozen steps, he considered all the things he had never done in his life, wondering if he would have a chance after this.

Gareth dropped to his knees and slid across the wet cobbles between the legs of the charging immortal. He thrust upwards with the obsidian sword, driving it into the belly of the beast and up through the middle of its back. The scream was horrifying, and he was sure it woke half of the city. He turned and looked behind him at the vampire as it stumbled through the rain, trying to hold on to market stalls to balance itself, but falling regardless. It laid there bleeding out as it wailed. The dark blood swirled in the rainwater, running between the cobbles like creeks running between tiny islands.

Chapter Eight

Almost a week had passed, and tomorrow night Gareth would meet with Hector. Since his encounter with the vampire in the market, he had been somber. He knew the thing wasn't human, or even alive, but he still felt like he had killed for the first time. He looked down at his hands in the firelight of the Lusty Mermaid's tap room, almost expecting to find blood on them even after so many days.

Marcella walked by, brushing subtly against his shoulder as she made her way to wait on a table. She had been kind to him during the last few days. He had drunken heavily that first night, but his consumption had been tempered since then. She didn't understand why he had been so glum, and he wasn't willing to tell her. She had accepted that he had problems and left it at that, considering that he was handling things better than the last time she had seen him so troubled.

He had gone to the Two Fishes a few times, as well. It was good to spend time around Fergus again, now that he didn't have to worry about the big man crushing his skull. Nikolai had been teaching him things that might help him in his upcoming confrontation. Gareth reached behind him and softly touched the blade of the obsidian sword. Despite his victory in the market, he still felt ill prepared to face Gisella.

The female vampire had been his first real encounter with their kind. Despite his civil discourse with Hector and the defeat of the nameless immortal, the memory of Gisella giving chase that night still terrified him. The fire in her eyes frightened him the most. She had not been angry, nor had she been methodical. She had enjoyed the chase. The woman was a born killer, and she had reveled in every moment of the pursuit.

Gareth stood and walked over to where Jacob was behind the bar. The proprietor of the Lusty Mermaid was a cheerful fellow with an easy smile and kind features. The old sailor had gotten soft since settling down to run the tavern. He was not fat, but not thin either. Jacob wore simple woolen clothes despite the wealth he must have amassed over the years. Wealth which, per some personal code, Gareth had left undisturbed. Spilled drink and vomit stained Jacob's apron, although he took pains to clean it regularly. At one time it had been a vibrant white, a costly piece of fabric, but now it was a dingy yellow. The man had thin brown hair cut short, and a bushy mustache above a shaved chin and clean cheeks. Gareth laid a few coins down on the bar. Jacob's eyes widened, as the pile was more than was owed, and a single gold coin sat twinkling in the middle of them.

"You buying a room permanently?" Jacob asked.

Gareth shook his head, his eyes averted, "No, just consider it gratuity for many years of friendship and strong drinks."

"Something's bothering you. You can talk to old Jacob, you know," Jacob said, referring to himself in the third person. It was a habit he had when trying to talk somebody into opening up about their troubles or leaving without a fight.

"No," Gareth said, "I can't. Not this time. Thank you, Jacob."

Gareth walked out of the tavern into the crisp evening air. The sun had just set, so as he was leaving most of the Maid's patrons would be on their way in to start a night of drink and reverie. He hoped he would be able to join them in a day's time, but for now he wasn't in the mood for merry-making. His feet took him through the city slowly. He wondered as he passed every building if this would be the last time he would ever see it. Memories of rooftop chases, daring leaps, and fat purses all floated through his head. *Until now,* he thought, *it seems like my life has meant nothing.*

Tomorrow, that might change. He was setting out to rid the city of a terrible threat. He imagined himself standing atop a carriage in a parade, crowds cheering him and women flashing their breasts, hoping to garner his affection. He saw children dressing up like him and playing Gareth and Gisella in the streets. Sadly, though, the battle would take place in the shadows where he had lived his entire life. There would be no parade and no adoring public. He preferred it that way. He didn't like attention or crowds, so the daydream made him shudder some. Except for the breasts;

he liked that idea. One thing to look forward to if I survive, he thought, then corrected himself: Two.

He stopped by to see Miles, his favorite street urchin. The boy was behind the blacksmith shop as usual, joined by some other waifs. They were some of Gareth's sparrows, so he knew them all by name. The girl was Hatha, only six years old, but she already had sharp eyes. Her curly blond hair and innocent face made her an ideal cutpurse. Nathan was almost as tall as Miles, but broader and more muscled. They were the same age; both having seen fourteen summers. Where Miles was quick and agile, Nathan was strong and sturdy. The boy could fell a goat with one punch, and one day would graduate to horses. The last was Liam, a quiet boy with jet black hair curled tight about his head. His olive skin bespoke of him being the orphan of foreigners, probably a merchant from some southern nation who had failed to make a name for himself here. Liam was a bit of a mystery to Gareth, but the eight-year-old boy was a good sparrow and could get into and out of almost anywhere without being seen.

Gareth spent some time talking to them, garnering a little of the city's gossip but mostly just enjoying their company. The children really were becoming a family with one another, and his role as their mentor and benefactor filled him with pride. He handed out treats and coin, more than usual, and thanked them for helping him. They looked at him with confused expressions; all but Miles. The young man was sharper than most at his age, and he knew when something was amiss. As Gareth walked out of the alley, Miles gave chase.

"Something's up," he said.

Gareth stopped and turned, frowning down at the boy. He didn't want to trouble them. Nikolai had warned him not to talk of the vampires. To expose their secret would be to create a long list of potential victims, nothing more. On top of that, most people wouldn't be able to process the news. Even Gareth, somewhat learned thanks to Helen, had difficulty dealing with his new awareness despite his own confrontations with the undead. "Something's always up."

"No," Miles said, poking a finger at the man's chest, "you've been acting weird. You're in trouble, and I want to help."

Gareth smiled. Miles really was turning out to be very much like himself, but he was still too young for this sort of endeavor. "Not yet," he said, and he turned to walk away.

Chapter Nine

It was well past sunset before Gareth left his house. He had been gazing at the goblets again and lost track of time. He put the fireplace back together, but had left a scrap of parchment sticking out from underneath the loose stone. If he did not return, he hoped that Miles would find the note that he had written.

The rain had returned in force, and the streets already flowed with the typical mixture of water and refuse. It wasn't deep yet, but given time the deluge would be severe. Gareth wondered if the rain could wash the sorrow from the city along with the grime. So many of his fellows suffered under the yoke of poverty, not even knowing that they were also food for immortal predators. And the knowledge that those who held the power in the city, those who were clutching the proverbial purse-strings, were also those using the people like livestock infuriated him.

He did not bother to take to the rooftops, not tonight. His mission, though clandestine, did not require such nimble acrobatics. By the time he reached the Noble Quarter, that mode of travel would be impossible. The water sloshed around his feet as he slogged through the Merchant's Quarter. Rain dripped from the edge of his hood and ran in chilly rivulets down the front of his shirt. He was not discomfited by the water or the chill, however. His mind was elsewhere.

He had made his preparations. If he died tonight, he would not have things he wished to say. At least, not things that he could say. He had spent the morning at the orphanage with Helen and the children. He brought toys from Brachus to them, ones that he actually purchased from the carver with coin that came not from his own coffer. He also left a substantial anonymous donation secreted into Helen's dresser drawer in the form of a purse full of silver coins. Finally, he had left the note to Miles, explaining everything that had happened over the last month and beseeching him to seek out Nikolai. There was also mention of what lie under the loose stone, and the documentation to transfer ownership of the hovel to the boy.

Feeling confident that there was nothing more to be done, he allowed his feet to carry him to the Noble Quarter. His own weight seemed to drag him down as he climbed the hill, something more in his head than his muscles. His pace slowed, and he took a circuitous route to the estate. He wanted this night to be over, but he was in no hurry to face what was to come.

His only hope, ironically, lie with Hector. If the vampire doubled-crossed him, there would be nothing that he could do against the two of them. He might get lucky and kill one, but with their unnatural speed there was no way he could slay both at once. Even facing Gisella alone, in her joyful ferocity, he knew that he could not succeed without Hector's aid.

He turned a corner, and the immortal on his mind appeared before his eyes. The man was standing there by the wall of some noble estate, perfectly still. *How long had he stood there without moving?* Gareth wondered. His features were placid, and even the tail of his long coat was serene despite the wind and rain. It was not natural, and seeing such stillness amid the ferocity of the storm made Gareth's head swim. Lightning flashed over the city, and an ominous thunder rolled long and loud. The lightning lit up the features of Hector's face. Saying that he was pale would have been accurate to describe his visage, but inadequate. Gaunt would be appropriate, yet understated. As he approached, Gareth could see veins in Hector's hands, neck, and face. They seemed flushed with blood. His skin was slightly translucent, revealing a hint of what lie beneath.

"Our arrangement stands?" Gareth asked.

"It does," Hector replied.

"How are we doing this?" Gareth got right to the business at hand.

Hector turned and motioned with one outstretched arm for Gareth to walk with him. The vampire's cloak hung over that arm, still not moving in the wind.

Gareth walked with him.

"I have arranged a…" Hector hesitated, searching for the word, "gift for my sister."

Gareth nodded, paying close attention.

"She will be feeding, her senses focused on the kill. This is the only time she may be distracted enough for you to approach her. I know you already slew one of us, but she is much faster and much stronger than that one was."

Gareth stopped, his hand drifting to the obsidian sword.

Hector held out a hand, "Tss, no. I feel no need of vengeance. Doran was simply hunting, and you his prey. Unluckily for him, his prey won out that night. It is a risk we face, always."

"So, this…"

"Doran."

"Doran. He was not as strong or as fast as Gisella? I barely beat him," Gareth was crestfallen. That former victory was where the little confidence he had about tonight was coming from.

"No, not by any means. Understand, Gareth, that we grow stronger with age. The more we learn, the more we feed, the more powerful we become. Doran was human merely a decade ago. He was a merchant, and a successful one. He sought position on the council, and a price is to be paid for membership."

"Wait, are you saying that the entire council is immortals?" Gareth asked.

Hector looked at him, his face still betraying no emotion, but one eyebrow cocked in curiosity.

"Nikolai did not figure this out? No, that's not it," he smiled, "he didn't tell you."

Gareth thought on this for a moment, not wanting to consider Nikolai had held anything back, but finding it hard to believe that the man had missed such a key detail. "Why?"

Hector smiled again, holding his hands before him as if he were holding a hand of playing cards. "Not tipping his hand, as you say."

Gareth laughed at the gesture, which seemed so strange from the foreign immortal, but then he grew serious. "Wait, if Doran was a vampire for only a decade, how long have you and Gisella been immortal?"

Hector cringed at the use of the word vampire, but understood the human's slip of the tongue. "Centuries," he said without further illumination.

Gareth frowned. He couldn't even imagine how powerful these two were, considering he barely survived the confrontation with Doran in the market. He could only hope that Hector's plan would play out. It bothered him; this talk of a 'gift.' He knew that could only mean some hapless soul from the city was being handed over to the vampire bitch, so he would have a chance to stab her in the back. Even in stopping her from killing, an innocent had to die. The irony almost outweighed the tragedy of it all.

He shook the thoughts from his mind as they approached Hillcrest Manor. He had not seen the estate for some time, and the ominous facade made him tremble. Hector glided up to the gate, still unmanned, and inserted a slender key into the lock. He swung open the iron bars, inviting Gareth inside before locking it behind them.

"Still having staffing issues?" Gareth joked, trying to calm his own nerves.

"Yes. Gisella has created a poor reputation for us as employers," Hector explained.

Gareth nodded.

"I will fetch her. The gift is in the garden, and you will find ample options for places to seclude yourself. Be as still as possible and wait until she has begun to feed before you strike."

"I'd ask you to wish me luck, but I'm not sure if you people believe in such a thing."

Hector smiled, "We make our own luck. Strike true and fast, and be sure that you must only strike once, for that will likely be the only chance you have." With that, the old vampire walked up to the main entrance of the manor.

Gareth crept around the side of the building, passing the window to the library that now had the curtains
drawn. He saw the flicker of candlelight from within
and from the room he knew to be the parlor. There
might be servants inside, even if they couldn't hire
guards, or Gisella might be just on the other side of that
wall. His heart raced; the mere possibility of her close-
ness terrifying him.

He saw the 'gift' in the garden, a man of only eight-
een years. He was bound and gagged, and he looked
wide-eyed at Gareth as he struggled to beg for help
around the cloth. Gareth's heart leaped to his throat,
choking him. Here was this man pleading for salva-
tion, seeing Gareth as a potential rescuer. Meanwhile,
he planned to watch from the shadows as Gisella mur-
dered this man and made a meal of him. He knew that
killing her would prevent many more such deaths, including his own, but he could not help to feel guilty for
standing by while this man perished.

Despite the darkness, he found a circle of rose
bushes in full bloom and thick with green leaves. In the
center was a slender elm tree. He pushed his way
through the bushes, grimacing as thorns tore through
his clothes and into his flesh. He crouched down in the

small space between the flowers and the tree and waited.

Several minutes later Hector and Gisella entered the yard from a side door. Gareth presumed it was a room behind the parlor, or maybe a hallway. He was curious to see the rest of the manor, but at the same time wished that he didn't know as much about it as he did. The two vampires crossed the yard, hand in hand, laughing with one another. Hector looked charming, and under any other circumstances he would appear to be a dashing youth leading his lady to the dance floor of a ballroom. Now, he was leading his own sister to her death. Uncannily, despite the continued downpour, they both appeared to be bone dry.

Gisella's face bore a broad smile, and Gareth was entranced by it. If he hadn't been so terrified of the woman, he would feel urges about her stronger than he had felt for any other. She wore a new dress this time, and again it was red. The dress was satin and shined in the torchlight from the side of the building, the bell-shaped skirts swaying as she walked. While Hector's clothes and hair seemed to defy all rules of motion, her dress and her fiery red hair flowed around her with a fluid grace that made her look like she was doing some dance under the sea. The contrast in the two was remarkable, and it made Gareth nauseous. The way they moved, each in their own way defying any natural law, was difficult for the senses to comprehend.

Hector led her to the man bound atop a circle of paving stones in the garden. There was a bench there, a nice place for one to sit and enjoy the sun if such an activity would not cause their demise. Under the cloud enshrouded moon, the two of them walked gaily through the open air. Hector seated himself as Gisella approached her victim. The rain-soaked man looked up at them, terrified, and then looked towards the roses that hid Gareth.

Damn! Gareth thought. I shouldn't have let him see me.

He was lucky, though, that Gisella seemed uninterested in what her meal was looking at. Hector looked his way though, a look of consternation on his face. Gareth had almost ruined everything in his carelessness. The woman danced around her prey, laughing and singing. She was taunting the man. It was as if she were feeding on his fear as an appetizer before the entrée of his life's blood. She beamed, enjoying every moment, and her long fangs dripped with saliva.

Gareth's pulse was pounding. She may have enjoyed the anticipation, but it nearly drove him mad. He wished she would just get it over with, so he could either kill her or she him. One way or the other, only one of them would live to see the dawn.

Oh, that's ironic, he thought. He would have laughed, were he not terrified.

Finally, she bent over her prey with a speed that defied any logic. Had Gareth blinked at that moment, it would have been as if she had moved instantly from one place to the other. She hissed softly and dug her teeth into his neck, just above the collarbone. The man struggled, but soon fell still. Even through the gag, Gareth could hear him moaning in some perverted mixture of pleasure and pain. Hector's eyes were focused on the roses.

Gareth pushed out of the bushes as quietly as he could and walked up behind the woman. He slid the obsidian sword from the sheath on his back slowly and held it out before him. He had killed Doran in self-defense, struggling for his own life. He knew that Gisella would kill him just as surely, but to stab the woman in the back felt like murder to him. Gareth hesitated only momentarily, but it was long enough. Gisella stopped feeding and her head cocked to the side as she sniffed the night air.

"Now!" Hector yelled, raising his voice for the first time that Gareth had heard.

Gareth plunged the sword into her back, feeling the blade slide between ribs and tear through skin, muscle, and organs. Her scream pierced the darkness, a wail so hideous that it would haunt the dreams of all who slumbered in the city that night. Gareth yanked the sword free, readying it for another strike.

Gisella turned and was upright before him faster than he could adjust his grip on his weapon, teeth bared and hissing. Black, tarry blood oozed from a wound under her breast where the point of the sword had passed through. He had run her through, but missed the heart. She might die from the cut, but not before she killed Gareth in return.

He thrust the sword again, aiming directly at her heart, but she seemed to vanish and was suddenly standing beside him. She backhanded him across the face, a contemptuous blow intended to wound, but not kill. He flew back and fell hard to the ground, the obsidian sword falling from his hand. So, this is it, he thought, certain that his next breath would be his last. He looked up at that flowing red hair, waving around her like a halo of fire as she raced towards him with talon-sharp fingers outstretched. Just before she reached him there was a blur of black that threw her to the side.

Gareth drew another breath, one more than he had expected to, and another after that; shocked to be alive. He heard screaming and saw Gisella lying on the ground with Hector's arms wrapped around her. He struggled to hold her. Gareth reached for his sword and stood. Everything seemed to stand still for a moment. Gisella and Hector grappled nearby, and the man bound in ropes gasped for air as he bled out on the paving stones. Lightning flashed and thunder boomed as the rain poured from the sky. To Gareth everything was silent, calm, and peaceful. For just a moment, the world seemed to stop moving and became complete serenity. He took three steps towards the vampire siblings, held up the sword, and plunged it through the center of Gisella's chest.

Again, that horrible scream shot through the city, but it was brief. Sound and motion returned, and Gareth fell to his knees, panting. The sword stood in the woman's chest, like some monument on a field of battle. Hector laid her down gently, closing her eyes with two fingers and kissing her forehead; the act reminding Gareth he had just killed this man's sister.

"I'm sorry," he said.

"Do not be, Gareth," Hector replied solemnly. "She was my sister, but she became a monster. It had to be done."

"Hector?" Gareth hesitated.

The vampire looked up at him.

"Why couldn't you do it?" he asked.

Hector looked down at the body of his sister, stroking that wavy red hair. "Could you kill your sister, if you had one? There is no code, no mystical explanation…" He looked Gareth in the eye. "I was too weak to carry out the deed myself. Thank you."

Chapter Ten

Gareth groaned and shifted in the chair, the bruises all over his body making it hard to find any comfortable position. The fire was warm, though, and felt good on his bare feet. He scratched them on the straw rug. It hurt too much to bend down to reach them due to his broken ribs.

Helen frowned at him from her chair, worry on her face. He had been there for a week already, and still was constantly in pain. He wouldn't tell her all that had happened. He said it was a brawl at the Lusty

Mermaid, but she doubted that. He had never been hurt this badly before, and she knew he wasn't telling her something.

He smiled at her, trying to hide a grimace of pain as he reached for the steaming mug of cider. He took a sip of the delicious apple brew, letting it trickle down his throat slowly. She had always found the best cider and mulled it herself with cloves and sticks of cinnamon. The smell filled the sitting room, mixing with the smoke of the wood burning in the fireplace. It smelled like home to Gareth. No matter how much time passed or where he may lay his head at night, this place would always be home.

*　　*　　*

A week later, he stood before a fire in another hearth. He was back in his little shack. Firelight gleamed from his polished boots and the hearth's heat fanned the cloak falling from his shoulders. He held a scrap of paper in his hand, a hasty note scrawled upon it. He read the note that he had left for Miles one last time, then tossed it into the fire. "Not yet," he said, and walked out into the darkened street.

He made his way to the rooftops, and to the gazebo over the bell tower. He looked out over Seahaven, his city. He didn't feel like some hero of the people, or even their protector. He was just a man, and he had only done what was necessary. He was glad things were back to normal, even though he knew that there were other creatures of the night out there. Some of them, he imagined, were prowling in the shadows just as he was, but with more nefarious designs. He would keep living, though. Live until somebody stops you, Kholas always said. It was a simple maxim, but a good one. We all will die one day, but until then all you could do was make the best of the hand dealt to you.

Gareth walked to the edge of the roof and jumped off, grabbing the rope stretched across the gap between the buildings, and climbed hand over hand across the empty space. He dropped onto a balcony and quietly pulled open the window. Soft snoring came from inside, and he slipped in like a shadow flitting across a wall.

He opened the wardrobe and deftly pried loose the panel from the bottom. Inside was the box he expected to find, and inside that a pouch of coins. He hefted it in his hand and realized it was heavier than usual. He opened it to look inside and found it mostly full of silver, with some twinkling gold coins peeking out here and there. *Where did he get this kind of coin?* Gareth thought. He kneeled there before the wardrobe for several long minutes, considering what to do. He never felt guilt stealing from the fat cats of the city, but this was a fortune.

"Take it," a voice said from across the room.

Gareth stood sharply, his hand going to his dagger. There, sitting on the edge of the bed, was Brachus. The wood carver smiled at him, holding his hands out to show that he was unarmed. "Go ahead," he said again, "take the bag."

"No," Gareth said, "I can't."

"You never hesitated before," Brachus said, smiling.

Gareth paused. So, the man knew he had been robbing him all along.

Brachus saw this in his face and chuckled, "Why do you think I charge so much for my wares? You thought I was just greedy? I always considered it a tax, payable to Helen's orphanage. You're just the tax collector."

Gareth shook his head, amazed that the man had let him steal from him for years. He looked back down at the bag of coins. "This is too much."

"No, it's not. I have more stashed away, anyway. There are those of us among the merchants that know more than we let on, and we know what you did. Consider it a gratuity." Brachus winked and laid back down on the bed.

Gareth put the bag in his satchel, saying nothing more, and went to the window. Outside, on the balcony, he said aloud to himself, "You know what that means?"

He closed the widow behind him, smiling. "I haven't found Brachus' real stash yet!"

The end, for now...

Gareth's story continues, and that of Miles begins, in

The Hunter's Apprentice

The Ravencrest Chronicles
Book Two

Miles grew up as an orphan in Seahaven. The coastal city has always been his home, and the streets have always been where he laid his head. Now he's learning the shadow craft from his mentor, Gareth. But when Miles uncovers secrets behind a sinister plot, he discovers there are deadlier things awaiting in the shadows than he could have imagined. And with Gareth's help, he must learn to hunt them down.

Continue reading on the next page for a special preview of the first chapter of *The Hunter's Apprentice*!

The Hunter's Apprentice

Chapter One

Miles padded silently through the shadows of the back alley, his bare feet making nary a sound. Both moons were full tonight, but there was darkness enough in the tight confines of the city streets for him to hide in. He found the door he was looking for and smiled a crooked smile. A few teeth were missing, a reminder to avoid a fight when one could. He crouched down before the door, his knee wet in a puddle where his wool trousers were ripped and torn. He shook his unruly mop of dirty blond hair, blowing a few loose strands away from his eyes. The door had an iron lock set into it, but that would not be a problem for the young thief. Miles reached into a pocket and fished around for his steel picks, which had been a gift from his mentor. He deftly inserted the picks into the lock, feeling for the tumblers and setting them into place one by one. There were four in all, a complicated lock for this part of the city, but in no time, he had the door open. Sliding inside unseen and unheard, he softly pressed the door closed behind him.

The back room of the shop was unremarkable, with stacks of crates and an odd barrel here and there. The smell of salted fish was heavy in the storeroom of the butcher's shop, made that much more acute by the smell of smoke from a fire in the next room. There was a brick chimney there that formed a cylinder in the center of the room. At the bottom was a large space for a fire, and above were racks and hooks for smoking meat behind a heavy iron door. The chimney was full of all sorts of mutton, pork, and fish; even at this hour of the night. There would be hungry bellies in Seahaven in the morning, and the butcher was sure to have smoked herring ready for the breakfast rush.

Miles, however, would not wait that long. He found several parchment sheets and bundled some of the more done looking pieces of fish from the chimney, adding a few crabs for good measure. He took as much as he could carry, and considering he was an athletic sixteen-year-old, that was a pretty good haul. Filling a burlap sack with the parchment bundles, he headed over to the counter in the next room. This was where Haemish the butcher would greet his customers in a few hours. Below the counter was a small coffer. Miles knew this was not the meat vendor's treasure trove, but the spare coin would be enough. There was a silver piece in there, a few copper coins, and a handful of copper bits. Enough for some drink for everybody, with some to spare.

Miles smiled that crooked smile, his missing teeth making it just that much more charming. His bronzed skin, dark from spending so much time in the summer sun, glistened with sweat as he walked back by the fire and towards the rear door to the shop. Silently he passed through the portal and made his way back down the alley and out to the street. Two-story building surrounded him, almost all of them of daub and wattle construction with cobblestone foundations.

There were a few pieced together with wooden plank, but this was rare.

The sun would rise over Seahaven soon. The predawn glow was visible out towards the harbor district. From where he was on Trader's Way in the Mercantile District, Miles could see all the way down the hill to the ocean. The principal thoroughfare of the city was broad and open, one of the few streets that did not make one feel like they were being smothered by the surrounding buildings. The cobbles of the street were even, smooth, and well maintained. The hill rose sharply from the sea into the Noble Quarter, where the road twisted and turned to make the ascent manageable. In this part of the city there were great stone manors surrounded by protective walls.

In the other direction was the harbor, beyond the sprawl of the city. Trader's Way cut a neat path through the center of it all and looked like a scar dug out of the landscape. All around it were mazes of side streets and back roads lined with shanties, shacks, and hovels. Some of the homes and businesses were quite nice, and there were even several with log walls instead of plank. But most of them consisted of rough timber and wood planks, with roofs of tree bark shingles or thatch. It was here in Shanty Town that most of the residents of Seahaven struggled to survive.

Beyond was the harbor itself, lined with docks which hosted an array of sailing ships. There were two-masted schooners bound for local ports, three-masted carracks ready to travel abroad, and even strange caravels and galleys from faraway lands. All there for the one thing that made Seahaven more than just another fishing village on the coast: coin. Seahaven was a trade port. Goods and coin flowed into and out of the city daily. Most of the people of Seahaven, though they might labor at one enterprise or another, never saw much of that coin.

Up the hill it went, and the aristocracy hoarded most of it there. The middle-class merchants ended up with a comfortable share, but even their fat bellies and jingly purses paled compared to the coffers of the Noble Quarter. Beyond that, atop one of the two soaring cliffs that bracket the city and Bleakstone Bay, sat Castle Ravencrest. This was the home of the so-called lord of Seahaven, Duke Piotr. He rarely made public appearances, leaving the bureaucracy of the city to the Council of Barons. And thus had life in Seahaven always been, and so it would always be. Miles sighed as he looked up at the castle on the bluff, wondering what it was like inside. *Maybe one day I'll break in and rob the place,* he thought. Laughing at the notion, he continued to make his way down into Shanty Town.

The sun had peeked over the horizon and he could hear the gulls crying their morning calls. The sea sparkled green and blue under the light, and long shadows from the masts of sailing ships drew lines over Shanty Town. Miles came down the hill to the clustered shacks he called home, and the shadows between them soon sheltered him. He wove his way along the twisting alleys, cobbled streets giving way to packed dirt. The people of Shanty Town were rising with the sun, and he usually got a wave and a smile as he passed by. The city of Seahaven was large, and nobody could know every soul within its stone walls, but Miles was close to home and the community here was tight-knit. He waved to Loden, the blacksmith, as he pivoted down a narrow path between his shop and the next building. He tossed the sack down next to a large bale of hay and pulled a filet of smoked fish from a bundle of parchment. He jumped on top of the hay and nibbled at the fish, savoring the smoky and salty flavors. The hay was there for Nance, who was Loden's donkey. Nance's job was to walk in a circle, turning a large wheel attached to the blacksmith's bellows. It was a marvelous contraption that saved Loden and his apprentices time and effort and kept the fires of the forge hot all-day long. In return, there was always fresh hay and carrots for Nance. Loden kept the carrots inside, though.

Loden tolerated having Miles living in the alley behind his shop, and in return Miles kept an eye out for the blacksmith and drove off any would-be thieves. Sure, Miles was a thief, but he didn't steal from Loden, and that was all that concerned the burly blacksmith. Miles had been living on the streets for almost five years, since his ma and pa mysteriously disappeared. That happened a lot in Seahaven, especially to the poor. People would go about their business one day, and the next they would be gone.

Miles could have gone to stay at the orphanage with Helen, but he liked it out here on the streets. He wasn't much of a people person, except for a close group of friends, so the mere thought of being in the big house with all those brats made him queasy. He would rather be on his own, make his own rules, and find his own way. He did well for himself, truth be told. He was rarely hungry and often had a few coins jingling around in his pocket. Much of this was due to his intrepid enterprises like this morning's trip to the meat market, and much of it was due to his shadowy benefactor.

Miles was a sparrow.

One might hear that word and imagine an insignificant creature that flits about silently. They might think of something that cocks its head, watching and listening, and that takes flight at the first sign of trouble. A tiny thing that, in the right moment, may chirp and sing for you. If they were thinking about a bird, they would be wrong.

Miles was a sparrow, as were many of his friends. Street urchins and poor waifs—every one of them—the sparrows were the eyes and ears of the most renowned thief in all of Seahaven: Gareth Vann. They would hide in plain sight, watching and listening. Their hungry eyes ensured that nobody with half a copper looked at them, lest they feel the pang of guilt at not helping the poor soul. They were dirty little scoundrels, skilled at a variety of nefarious tasks.

Gareth would come with sausages, biscuits, pastries, and coin. He would ask them, "Little sparrow, what's new today?" And so, his birds would sing to him; and he would know who had been where, with whom, and what they were doing. And if there were coin changing hands, or goods being smuggled, Gareth knew about it; because the sparrows saw it happen or heard that it was about to.

Miles was not only a sparrow, he was one of the oldest. He had known Gareth for a few years now, but in the last several months the man had begun teaching him more and more of the shadow craft. He had given him the picks and taught him their use. He had even given Miles a small dirk, barely a hand span long, to defend himself with. He always had it with him, in a battered sheath hidden under his baggy shirt.

The shadows were shortening as the sun rose, and it surprised Miles that none of the other sparrows had stopped by yet. They knew he had been planning to gather food, so they should show up. Just as he was thinking this, the first of them rounded the corner. Naturally, it was Nathan. The burly young man was the same age as Miles, but had twice the appetite. They were the same height, but Nathan was broad of stature and heavily muscled, while Miles was lithe and agile. His friend was the thug of the bunch, and although he was not as discreet as the other sparrows, he had his uses when somebody needed their skull thumped.

"Nathan, good morrow!" Miles called out, reaching into the sack and throwing a parchment wrapped bundle of fish to the other boy.

Nathan struggled clumsily to catch the bundle, cursing under his breath, and shot an annoyed glare at Miles. "Could have just handed it to me, you little bugger."

"No fun in that. How would I get to see you flailing about like your breakfast did when it was pulled into the boat?" Miles was laughing so hard he had to hold his belly.

Nathan shoved an entire fillet in his mouth and said, "I gmph mphk mur amphs." Bits of flaky fish fell out of his mouth, sticking to his puffy lips. He smiled, showing off even more of his half-eaten breakfast.

"Gross, tell him to stop," a girl said.

Miles looked over and there was Hatha, standing right next to him. He would swear that even if he had been looking, she still would have sneaked up on him. The little curly-haired blond with blue eyes could stand out in a crowd if she wanted to, or she could creep up on a door mouse without being heard. Either way, she made for the perfect cutpurse. Either you saw her and thought she was too adorable to do any harm, or you never even knew she was there.

"Okay, Nathan, that's enough," Miles admonished his friend.

Nathan wiped his mouth with the back of his arm and said to Hatha, "I'm sorry."

Just then, Miles heard a crunching noise and looked down from the hay bale to see Liam standing over his bag, cracking open one of the smoked crabs. "When did you get here?"

The bronze skinned child shrugged his shoulders and stuffed a bit of crab meat into his mouth. His dark skin and tight, curly hair stood in testament to Liam's southern origins. His parents had probably come to

Seahaven hoping to make their fortune. His presence in the alley spoke of their success at that endeavor. The boy was an exceptional sneak, and this was not the first time he had surprised Miles like this. The young boy didn't say much, but when he did, it was usually worth listening.

"Well," a gruff voice said, "looks like you're all eating well this morning."

Miles looked up and saw his friend and mentor, Gareth Vann, strolling down the alley. The man was in his thirties and maintained an exemplary physique. He wore his trademark dark cloak, jacket, pants, and knee-high boots. The hilts of daggers peeked out from his coat, along with a short bow and a quiver of arrows hanging at his hip. Miles knew as well that there was a sword beneath the man's cloak, carved of gleaming black obsidian and razor sharp. Gareth did not use it often, and he talked about it less. He rubbed his square chin covered in dark stubble and said, "I don't suppose you have any more of that smoked fish?"

Miles smiled up at his old friend and said, "Well, isn't this a change? Usually we're having to tell you the news to get food from you. Now you're hoping for a handout?" They all laughed at the irony except Liam, who remained quiet as usual.

"How about a trade?" Gareth asked, producing a cloth-wrapped bundle. He opened it, revealing some sticky sweet rolls. They had surely come from Helen's kitchens at the orphanage. The eyes of the sparrows widened. They all knew how good Helen's sweet rolls were.

"Deal!" Nathan said.

"Dammit, Nathan, who taught you how to haggle?" Miles said.

"Obviously, not me," Gareth replied, smiling as he handed over the pastries and took his fish. "You've been doing well for yourself, I see."

Miles sat up straight, trying to look taller and prouder than usual, "Of course, I'm a master thief."

Again, there was a round of laughter from the sparrows. This time even Liam chuckled softly.

"Sure, you are," Gareth chided, "and I'm the master of the seas. Come on, we have business."

Miles glared at the others, who quickly silenced their mirth. "See? Business. He needs help from the master thief."

About the Author

B.K. Bass is the author of over a dozen works of science fiction, fantasy, and horror inspired by the pulp fiction magazines of the early 20th century and classic speculative fiction. He is a student of history with a particular focus on the ancient, classical, and medieval eras. B.K. has a lifetime of experience with a specialization in business management and human relations and served in the U.S. Army as a Nuclear, Chemical, and Biological Operations Specialist. When B.K. isn't dreaming up new worlds to explore, he spends his time as a bookworm, film buff, strategy gamer, and caretaker to an unusual number of cats and one small dog who thinks she's a cat.

Find out more and connect with B.K. at https://bkbass.com

Find *The Hunter's Apprentice* at bkbass.com!